D0932372

The Hitchhiker

a Dubois Files mystery

by Joan H. Young

cover illustration by Linda J. Sandow
interior illustrations by Joan H. Young

DUBOIS FILES BOOKS

DEDICATION

To the memory of my father,
Ray Ford Leary,
who told me to always carry
a stick to the woods

CORA'S INTRODUCTION

My name is Cora Caulfield, and I'm an older lady now. But when I was a child, my last name was Dubois. That's French, pronounced dew-BWAH. I've begun sharing these stories from my childhood with you.

Jimmie Mosher, Laszlo Szep, George and Ruby Harris, and I had an exciting month in June of 1953. We were country neighbors; we all lived on or near East South River Road, which is east of Cherry Pit Junction and south of the Petit Sable River.

Jimmie's family had been in danger of losing his farm to the bank, but we didn't give up looking for the paper that would prove the property had been paid for. I told that story in *The Secret Cellar*.

We thought that was an exciting way to begin summer vacation, but then a mysterious man appeared in July.

I first met the hitchhiker when my dad gave him a ride, but it took four of us to solve his problem.

BOOK TWO - THE HITCHHIKER

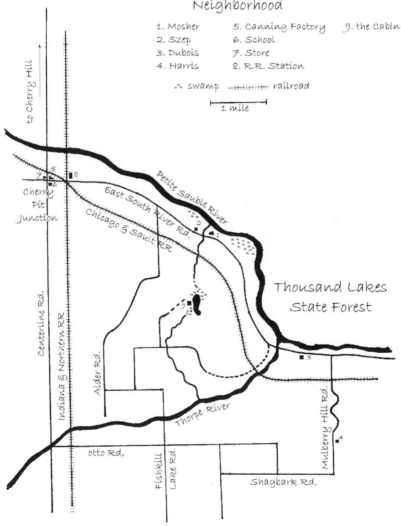

The East South River Road
Neighborhood

1. Mosher   5. Canning Factory   9. the Cabin
2. Szep   6. School
3. Dubois   7. Store
4. Harris   8. R.R. Station

swamp   railroad

1 mile

to Cherry Hill

Petite Sauble River

East South River Rd.

Chicago & Sault RR

Cherry Pit Junction

Centerline Rd.

Indiana & Northern RR

Thousand Lakes State Forest

Alder Rd.

Thorpe River

Mulberry Hill Rd.

Otto Rd.

Fishkill Lake Rd.

Shagbark Rd.

1. THE SPY IN BROWN

Cora Dubois was feeling crabby. She almost always got sick to her stomach if she didn't ride in the front seat. Nevertheless, she slid into the car's back seat, next to her mother, as she'd been told to do. She knew better than to be sassy and kept her thoughts to herself.

It was a pleasant afternoon in July, but Cora had spent almost the entire day in cars or buildings. She had been allowed to change out of her itchy church dress after Sunday dinner, but was told to put on a school dress for the afternoon. The family had driven to Fordberg, thity miles south of where they lived, to visit family friends. Friends of her father and mother anyway. There weren't any children there at all. Cora had found a book that looked interesting, and after politely answering too many adult questions, at least she'd been able to sit on the porch and read The Adventures of Robin Hood. It was an old book, but the friends didn't seem to have any newer ones for children. The cake was good, and she had been offered a cup of tea, which she liked, but her muscles ached to run and play.

Now they were on the way home, and her father decided to pick up the hitchhiker.

The man was standing at a crossroad. It was farther south than the area Cora was familiar with. He wore a suit, although it was rumpled. His necktie was straight, but the shirt collar was bent up on one side. An old brown leather satchel sat on the ground just below his left hand with a rolled-up brown plaid blanket tied across the top. He was resting all his weight on one leg, as if he'd been there a while and was tired. As the Dubois car approached, the man lifted his right hand toward the road and stuck out his thumb.

"What do you think, Reeta? He looks down on his luck, but hardly dangerous," Philippe Dubois said to his wife.

"All right," Cora's mother answered, "but put him in the front seat with you, so we can keep an eye on him."

And that was why Cora had to move to the back, in the middle of a day that already had been long and boring. The man might be interesting, though, even if she did have to sit in back.

But it turned out he spoke almost no English. Philippe tried to engage him in conversation as they continued north, but he just shook his head when Cora's father asked him what his name was or if he was looking for work.

He did point straight up the road and say slowly, "Serri Hillin."

"You need to get to Cherry Hill?" Philippe asked.

The hitchhiker nodded and leaned against the window. Almost instantly he fell asleep.

Cora was sitting directly behind the man, and she studied the back of his head. It was about all she could see of him. He had deep creases in the tanned skin of his neck, and they were full of dirt, like he hadn't washed in a long time. His suit was brown and smelled like old wool. His hair was light brown, too, but it was streaked with gray, and too long. He looked shaggy. When they'd first seen him he was wearing a brown fedora, but he'd taken that off when he had to bend almost double to get into the car. He was a tall man and older than her father, maybe as old as her grandfather. He must not have a home, or he would take a bath, Cora decided. Maybe he was a spy and didn't dare tell them his name. She decided to call him The Spy in Brown.

She dozed off too; that was the best way to keep from getting carsick and awoke when the car slowed. They weren't home yet, but her father had stopped at the corner of Centerline and Otto Roads.

"Wake up," Philippe said, shaking the hitchhiker gently, and then more forcefully.

The man groaned and lifted his chin from his chest where it had fallen. He seemed dazed.

"This is our turnoff. Cherry Hill is seven more miles, but we saved you quite a bit of walking." Cora's father pointed straight ahead.

Slowly the stranger opened the car door and unfolded himself from the seat. He lifted his valise from the floor of the car and set it outside. Then he stood up and fumbled to place the hat back on his head. Leaning down to peer inside, he nodded and smiled at everyone one by one and said, "Tanks, tanks." Then he turned and began walking slowly north on Centerline Road.

"That man looks ill," Reeta said.

"Perhaps, but he certainly didn't want our help," answered Philippe.

Cora thought she'd never been so disappointed at meeting a new person. But it wasn't the last time she saw the hitchhiker.

2. JIMMIE FOLLOWS THE CREEK

Jimmie Mosher was Cora's neighbor, as country neighbors go. They lived a little more than two miles from each other, on East South River Road. Jimmie's house was on the west side of the Thorpe River, and Cora's was on the east side. They both went to school in Cherry Pit Junction and were in the same grade.

But it was summer vacation now. The Fourth of July celebration was more than a week past. There had been a parade in Cherry Hill, candy and ice cream treats, pony rides and a greased pig race. Jimmie and Cora had both entered, but bigger kids had easily won. Even baby pigs were fast, not to mention slippery when smeared with lard.

The holiday had been a wonderful break from the everyday routine of chores. Jimmie's jobs included feeding the chickens and collecting eggs every day. There was drinking water to be carried from the barn pump and a trio of pigs to care for. The weeds in the garden seemed to appear overnight, and he was supposed to keep them hoed down so the vegetables could grow tall. It was a lot of work, but he was an only child, so he had no brothers or sisters who could share the responsibility.

For the most part, Jimmie didn't mind. He liked being outside. He liked how hard his muscles were from the work, and he knew that his jobs were important so the whole family could eat well.

***

Today, he hurried through his chores because he wanted to go exploring. His father, Jed Mosher, had told him there was a lake where the little creek that flowed through their property originated. Jimmie hadn't known this before. Although Jimmie's grandfather had built the house, Jimmie and his mother and father had only lived here a few months. Before that, their home had been in Shagway, a village in the next county to the west.

Immediately after lunch, Jimmie put on a long-sleeved shirt and his old sneakers that were a bit too small and had a hole in the toe. He slung a canteen full of water over his shoulder and headed for the workshop. His dad was sharpening a saw that was longer than Jimmie was tall. The file made screeching sounds as it rasped across the metal.

"Hi, Dad."

"Hello, son." Jed looked at Jimmie's clothes. "Do you have plans for the afternoon?"

"I'm going to follow our creek and find Fishkill Lake. The one you told me about."

"Chores done?"

"Yes, sir."

"Don't be late for dinner. You watch the sun. Three handwidths above the horizon will be about six- thirty.

"Sure, dad. I remember how to do that," Jimmie said. [1]

"One more thing," Jed added, nodding in the direction of the far wall but without stopping his work. "You take one of those walking sticks. It's prudent. You never know when a good stout stick might come in handy."

Jimmie grabbed a stick and set out to follow the creek. He smiled. He was being "prudent," and that sounded grown-up.

In about fifteen minutes, he made it to the railroad tracks where he and Cora had picked berries in June. There was almost a trail beside the creek for that distance. He and another good friend, Laszlo Szep, had also walked it for a second berry-picking, and animals followed the waterway as well.

But south of the train tracks there wasn't any sort of visible pathway. In fact, Jimmie had never followed the creek any farther. When they'd visited his grandparents, before they lived in this house, he hadn't explored far from the farm property. It seemed to Jimmie that he

---

[1] see how to estimate time with your hand at the end of the book

was much older now, even though, of course, only one year had passed since the previous summer. But he felt different--independent and confident.

The ground began to rise gently but surely on the other side of the tracks. There were no more berry bushes, but plants that loved water were plentiful. Patches of nettles tugged at his clothing, and he was glad he'd worn long sleeves even though the day was hot. Nettles had stinging hairs that made you itch for hours even though they didn't cause any serious harm.

Pretty soon, clumps of cattails appeared and without warning Jimmie's foot slipped into a soft spot, and water oozed over and through his canvas sneakers. By then, he was really hot, so the cool water felt refreshing on his feet. A few steps later he slipped in a muck hole and got wet to his knees. It wasn't too difficult to pull his feet out by bracing the walking stick on a dry spot, but the mud sucked at his shoes. He decided to be a little more careful about where he stepped.

From then on, he used the stick to test the ground before he took each step. In just a few minutes he could see open water ahead. The lake! At the same moment, he realized that everything else looked very much the same. Which way was home? He wasn't sure. Suddenly he wasn't feeling confident at all.

He decided to go to the lake. He was certain of that—he could see it. To his right the land seemed higher and drier. There were fewer cattails and more trees. That had to be good, so he angled that way.

Soon, he realized he was following a rise above the curve of the lake edge, and suddenly he entered an opening in the trees. A tiny shack with a small porch faced the clearing. The roof sagged and the porch floor had partially rotted away. Obviously no one lived here any more.

Even though he had no idea which direction to walk to return home, this shelter made him feel better, as if he'd arrived somewhere.

Jimmie carefully made his way around the holes in the porch and pushed open the door, which squealed on dry rusty hinges. The smells of dust and rodents filled his nostrils. Directly across from him was a bed, and in that bed was a man. His feet stuck out over the end of the bed, a brown fedora hung on a bedpost, and he was covered with a brown plaid blanket.

3. THE MAN IN THE BED

The man in the bed groaned and tried to sit up, but he was apparently too weak. He raised himself up on an elbow, turned his head and looked at Jimmie out of eyes that had sunk into his face. The deep shadows made his head look like a skull.

"Hey, mister, are you all right? Jimmie asked. He felt a little frightened, but the man seemed to be in trouble.

The man's eyes rolled upward, and he fell flat in the bed without saying a word.

Jimmie ran over and shook him, yelling, "Wake up, wake up. Are you OK?" The man was breathing, but he was burning with fever; his skin was hot and dry.

There wasn't much in the small room that was useful. Jimmie didn't see any other blankets. There was a small pot-bellied stove with no fire in it. A couple of open-faced cupboards stood against a wall. There was one table with a broken leg, and a single chair with a brown suit coat hung over the back. An empty bucket sat on the table. There wasn't any food, unless the man had some in the leather bag that lay open on the floor near the bed. Jimmie didn't think he should search through that. What if the man woke up and thought he was a thief?

There was still some water in Jimmie's canteen. Now he needed a cloth. The only thing he saw was a white shirt lying across the end of the bed.

"Please don't be mad, mister. I'm not trying to take your stuff," Jimmie said as he picked up the shirt. "But, you're really sick. I'm just going to cool you down like my mom does when I have a fever."

Jimmie moistened a sleeve with the water and wiped the man's face and forehead. His breathing was ragged, and he moaned a little.

"I have to get help," Jimmie told the man. "You need a doctor."

"No. No dok-tor," the man cried, swinging an arm wildly and almost hitting the boy.

"Jiminy Crickets!" Jimmie yelled. He jumped backwards two feet. "OK, but I need to get you some food, and more clean water. You stay here, and I'll be back."

As Jimmie ran out the door, he realized it was probably silly to tell the man to stay there, but it was the first thing that came to his mind. He almost fell through a hole in the porch floor in his hurry to get away. He jumped down the step and ran across the clearing, but then he remembered that he didn't know how to get home.

He also didn't have the walking stick or his canteen, but he wasn't going back inside. Not yet.

Looking around the edges of the clearing, Jimmie couldn't even find his own path. All he was sure of was that the lake had been on his left. The sun was high in the sky, so it wasn't as easy to figure out directions as it would be later in the afternoon when the sun would clearly be in the west.

He did find a linear opening that might have been an old driveway or road to the cabin, years ago. There were two shallow ruts about the right distance apart for car tires. Since they must lead to a road, Jimmie followed them.

He wasn't really scared that he might be lost. He knew he was only about a mile from home, and he'd either run into a road or the railroad tracks no matter which direction he went. He just hoped he'd recognize the road.

He walked fast, thinking. The cabin and the man might be about the same age. Maybe it was a place he'd lived when he was younger. But why had he come back? Was he looking for something he'd lost? What had made him sick?

Soon the ruts through the woods became dirt tracks and the tracks became a lane, and the lane grew in width until it was a narrow road. That road teed into yet another road. Jimmie still didn't know where he was, but he decided that if he'd walked most of the way around the small lake, a left turn should take him toward home.

The road crossed a small creek, but there was no bridge, only a culvert underground. This was not familiar either. Soon he began to jog. It was hard not to worry, although the road had to lead somewhere. But instead of becoming more traveled, it faded to ruts again and headed across a field. In the distance, Jimmie heard a train whistle. Suddenly, he was almost certain he knew where he was. He saw smoke from the steam engine as the train crossed far ahead of him. The train had passed before he reached the tracks, but now he knew for sure he was close to Cora's house.

He continued to jog, but the outgrown sneakers made his toes hurt so he slowed to a walk again. Every time he thought about the sick man in the bed he would speed up. He crossed the Thorpe River on the closed road bridge, waving to the men who were working on repairs, and reached the Dubois house out of breath and red-faced. Cora was sitting in the fork of a tree reading a book.

She jumped to the ground and pelted Jimmie with questions. "Jimmie Mosher, why are your legs covered with dried mud? And where's your bike? Did you run all the way here?"

"Almost," Jimmie said, answering only the last question. "What time is it anyway?"

4. PREPARE FOR NURSING DUTY

Jimmie was surprised that it was only two-thirty. A lot had happened since lunch, but there was still plenty of time before he had to be home. He explained about the sick man, and Cora said they had to help him right away. "We can pretend we're nurses."

"This isn't pretend, and anyway, boys aren't nurses," Jimmie answered.

"Don't be a drip," Cora said.

Reeta Dubois was also reading, although she was reclining in a lounge chair on the back porch. "Mom? Can Jimmie and I have a snack and some orange juice?" Cora asked her mother.

"Of course, dear. Do you need my help?"

"Oh, no, Mom. We can get it ourselves," Cora replied.

"Thanks a lot, Mrs. Dubois," Jimmie said politely.

"Perfect," Cora whispered as the two friends entered the kitchen.

"Yeah, we didn't have to lie. We only asked if we could have the food, not eat it." Jimmie grinned. "But I'll have a glass of water. I left my canteen in the cabin."

"Sure. Help yourself," Cora said. Have some crackers too.

Jimmie grabbed a glass from the cupboard and went to the small hand pump mounted over the kitchen sink. He worked the handle until cold clear water flowed, then he drank two full glasses and ate several graham crackers. Cora had one.

Cora filled her lunch-box thermos bottle with orange juice. They tried to decide what a really sick man could eat.

"I think we'll have to feed him," Jimmie said.

Cora added a spoon, cup, and dish to her lunch box. She went into the pantry and Jimmie followed.

"A can of applesauce would be good. And here's some chicken noodle soup," Cora said.

"My knife has a can opener on it," Jimmie boasted.

Cora nodded in response. "Is there any way to heat the soup?"

"There's an old stove. Maybe I can get it lit. It's like the one in my dad's workshop, but we'll need matches. "

"They're in the kitchen," Cora said.

"The lake water looked scummy, but with the stove going we can boil it to make it safe, and cook things, too. I saw a beat-up pan in the cupboard. Gee, I hope it doesn't have a hole. How about some oatmeal?"

Cora filled a plastic box with oatmeal flakes. She snuggled two eggs into the dry cereal. "With hot water we can poach the eggs. That's good for sick people. And tea. How much stuff do you think we can carry?" she asked, adding some tea bags to the pile. "My bike basket isn't very big."

"Do you have a rucksack?"

"No. Maybe we can tie some things in a blanket."

"That would work. There was only one in the cabin and he might need another at night."

They ended up stuffing a pillowcase with an old afghan, some worn out but clean washcloths, a towel, and a sheet.

"The sheet is easier to wash than a blanket if he throws up or something," Cora said.

Cora didn't own a canteen, and they thought they would need clean water right away, or in case the stove wasn't safe to use. The only container for drinking water they could find, that wasn't glass and that had a lid, was her mother's new Tupperware pitcher.

"Mom will kill me if we lose it," Cora said.

"We'll have to risk it," Jimmie said. "That's enough. Now we have to get all this out of the house."

"You take it out the front door. I'll go tell my mom we're going for a bike ride."

Jimmie smiled at Cora. "That's true. Just don't mention we only have one bike."

Cora felt bad for deceiving her mother, but the man had said, "No doctor." A parent would insist on that, so she and Jimmie were on their own. At least until something forced them to tell an adult.

They put the lunchbox and container of water in the bike basket. Cora sat on the handlebars holding the bulging pillowcase, and Jimmie pedaled the bike. It was going to be a long ride, Jimmie thought.

In fact, he wasn't quite able to manage it on the parts of the route that were just grassy lanes. He couldn't ride fast enough to balance the extra weight. For those sections Cora rode the bike and Jimmie jogged slowly beside her, his toes aching in the tight sneakers.

He easily remembered the way back to the cabin, and decided that even though it made several jogs, the graded parts of the route had to be Fishkill Lake Road.

Before they left the open road and entered the woods, Jimmie checked to make sure the sun was still high enough that he didn't need to worry about the time just yet. It was beginning to fall toward the western part of the sky, but he figured he had a couple of hours before he needed to head home.

Both children were so tired, and the track was so bumpy, that for the final approach to the cabin, they took turns pushing the bike. As they walked, they collected handfuls of small dry branches.

Entering the clearing, Jimmie looked around carefully now that he knew someone was inside. The outhouse door swung on one hinge, but the building seemed usable. The stovepipe chimney appeared to be sound, and although the roof sagged, there weren't any gaping holes. There was a small pile of split firewood stacked outside. It was very old, but dry. He checked, and most of it wasn't rotting. With the kindling they'd picked up it would be easy to get a fire going.

"Be careful on the porch," Jimmie said. "It's got a lot of holes."

Cora pulled the lunchbox and plastic water jug from her bike basket. Jimmie carried the pillowcase and the twigs, and he entered the cabin first.

"Hey, Mister, I came back with some food and things. This is my friend, Cora. She'll help." He stepped aside, and Cora could see the man in the bed.

Her eyes and mouth got round. "Oh!" she said, "it's The Spy in Brown."

5. THE PATIENT

The Spy in Brown was awake, but his eyes were too bright and they seemed out of focus. He was shivering.

"It's the fever—he's got the shakes," Cora said, taking charge.

She pulled the sheet and crocheted afghan from their bag and proceeded to re-make the bed around her patient. "This mattress smells awful." She wrinkled up her nose. "Jimmie, take the pillowcase and fill it with dry leaves or something soft for his head."

After Jimmie hurried outside to obey Cora's command, she filled the cup with orange juice and held it while the man took small sips.

"Would you like some applesauce?" she asked. The man drank some more juice and lay down without answering. He was soon asleep again.

Cora found the pan on the open shelves and washed it using as little of their clean water as possible. It didn't leak. Next, she held the empty pail up toward a window, and she couldn't see any spots of light that would reveal holes.

When Jimmie returned, they lifted the man's head and put the makeshift pillow beneath it.

"The bucket and pan are OK," Cora said. "I wish there was a broom."

"Well, there's not," Jimmie replied, being bluntly practical.

He opened the stove door and checked inside. No animal had built a nest there. He rattled the stovepipe and it held together.

"That's good," he said, "but I have to check the flue. Do you see any paper lying around?"

"There's newspaper shelf liner," Cora said.

"That'll be perfect."

Cora peeled up a page of the old news, although she was reluctant to burn up any kind of printed material. Jimmie opened the stove door, twisted the paper into a rope and lit a corner. As the fire licked into the yellowed newsprint, he held it inside the stove and watched the flames grow and pull up into the pipe.

"It's clear," he said, letting the paper drop into the stove before it burned his hand. "I think it's safe."

He placed the kindling and some of the wood in the bottom of the firebox, and lit the small twigs. A cheerful blaze was soon warming the bulging metal body of the stove.

"I'll get water from the lake," Jimmie said, picking up the bucket. "I'll try to find a place where there's no algae on top."

Cora followed him outside, planning to go with him. But a piece of twine tied to the porch railing was twisting in the light breeze and caught her attention. "You get the water. I've got another project," Cora said mysteriously. "I'll put wood on the fire."

"Suit yourself," Jimmie answered with a shrug. He swung the bucket in a circle and headed for the lake.

Cora kept her promise to feed the fire. It was strong enough now that she could add some bigger sticks that would burn longer. Then she untied the piece of twine, put it in her pocket, and went in search of some weed stalks that were about a foot long and fairly straight. When she had a big handful, she went back to the cabin and checked the fire again. It was burning nicely, and the cabin was getting too warm for a July afternoon. But she thought that was probably good for the sick man in the bed.

The straight twigs were not for the fire. Cora picked up Jimmie's walking stick and used the twine to tie the thin branches tightly in a circle around one end. She had made a broom.

When Jimmie returned with the full bucket, he found Cora happily sweeping out the cabin and banishing cobwebs. He shook his head in awe of his ingenious friend. He hefted the bucket on to the stove but had no idea how long it would take to boil that much water.

Cora filled the pan with clean water and set it beside the bucket. "If he wakes up, we can make some tea," she said.

Together they washed the tabletop and shelves, and Cora explained how she had met their patient and why she called him The Spy in Brown. She put the dish, spoon and cup on the clean table. They folded the towel and dry washcloths and arranged everything in the cupboards. This was like playing house, only much more serious. There was a real person who needed them.

Just then the man groaned and sat up. He said something that neither of the children understood. They couldn't even repeat the sounds he made, although it sounded like some language, rather than just random noises or grunts.

Cora held up a teabag for the man to see. He nodded, and she placed it in the cup and poured hot water over it from the pan. She held the cup out and the man took it in his large dirty hands.

He drank, slurping the tea and smacking his lips. He was still shaking.

Jimmie brought the cans of applesauce and soup to show the man. He pointed at the Campbell's Chicken Noodle. Jimmie quickly opened the can with the special blade on his knife. Cora refilled the man's tea and placed the soup in the pan with some clean water. Soon it was warm, and she carried the bowl and spoon to their patient.

He had been able to manage the cup, but the spoon was too much for him. He leaned against the wall, and Cora fed him the warm golden liquid.

"What's your name?" she asked, although her father hadn't gotten an answer to that question on Sunday.

The man said another string of syllables that made no sense.

"My Dad taught me a little French," Cora said. "Je m'apelle Cora."[2]   She pointed at

---

[2] My name is Cora, in French

herself. "Comment vous apellez vous?"[3] Then she touched the man with her finger.

The man pointed at Cora. "Co-ra," he said. Then he touched his chest and said, "Veli. Help Veli"

"Your name is Veli?" Jimmie said. "That's great. Now we know what to call you. What do you want us to help you do?"

But Veli poured out another group of senseless sounds.

"That's not French," Cora said. "Anyway, I don't know enough to be useful."

"Maybe it's Hungarian," Jimmie said. "Let's bring Laszlo here tomorrow. He'll know."

Just then a ray of sunlight shot through the upper corner of the western window. "Yikes! What time is it?" Jimmie yelled. He ran outside, looked at the sun, then came back in. "We have to go. Now," he said to Cora.

He turned to the man. "We have to go home, Veli, or we'll be in trouble. We'll come back tomorrow. There's water heating on the stove."

---

[3] What is your name, in French

"Maybe you'd like to wash up, or something. We brought you a towel, too, and more food." Cora added, pointing at the shelves.

The man nodded and lay back against the makeshift pillow. Pulling the blankets over his shoulder, he rolled to face the wall.

6. CANTEENS

Jimmie quickly pulled Cora's broom apart.

"I can't go home without the stick," he explained. He grabbed the canteen, took a drink, and then slung the narrow strap over his head and under his arm.

Cora protested. "But Veli will be thirsty when he wakes up."

She rinsed out the pan and poured the rest of the clean water in it, and she also filled the cup with orange juice and left it on the table. She folded the remaining newspaper pages and slipped them in her lunchbox to read later. They were old and fragile and almost broke along the folds.

The fire in the stove would go out, but the weather wasn't cold enough to need the heat for anything except cooking or boiling water.

"Can you find your way home all right?" Jimmie asked.

"Sure," Cora replied. "It's all roads for me. Can you?"

"Yeah, I know I'm west of the creek now, and the sun's low enough to be sure I'm going north if I keep it on my left. I'll either find the creek or the railroad tracks. But I'll have to hurry."

"We can't be late, or we'll never be allowed out tomorrow."

"Right," Jimmie said. "You're a brick, Cora. Thanks. I'll telephone you."

"You're not bad, yourself," she called over her shoulder, grinning, as she pedaled away.

Jimmie hot-footed it through the woods, staying on the high ground and heading steadily north. He reached the tracks, without encountering any more swamps or other problems, and then followed the rails east—to the right--toward the creek. He turned downstream and sprinted for home. There wasn't a lot of time to spare, but he washed quickly and slid into his chair at the dinner table just before six-thirty. He'd made it on time, but he was so tired he could hardly stay awake to eat. Much to his parents' astonishment, he went to bed right after dessert.

***

Cora was not so fortunate. Her mother met her as she rode into the front yard.

"Why did you take my new Tupperware pitcher on your bicycle?" Reeta Dubois asked. "And your lunch pail too. What are you up to?"

Cora had already planned her answer, just in case this happened. "I don't have a canteen like Jimmie does. I wanted to have water to drink when we got hot. I brought it home, Mom. It's not even dirty. "

"All right, Cora, but you should have asked."

Cora hung her head. "Yes, ma'am. And my lunchbox keeps things clean. It's last year's, so I thought it would be OK."

"That's fine, dear. It's yours. However, some things in the house are not."

Philippe had already returned home for the day from his work as manager at the canning factory in Cherry Pit Junction. He was seated in the living room reading the Cherry Hill Herald and looked up over the top of the paper as his wife and Cora entered the room.

"This little scallywag has been borrowing good kitchen containers for playing," Reeta said.

"What do you have to say for yourself, Cora?" Philippe asked gently.

"I'm sorry, Papa. I should have asked. But Jimmie has a canteen, and I only have my thermos bottle, which isn't very big, and the liner will break if I drop it. Anyway, it's old and smells like sour milk all the time."

"That is a problem," Philippe said, laying the newspaper aside. He winked at his daughter. "You wash up for dinner, and I'll be there in a minute."

Cora dragged her feet as she headed for the sink. She didn't like being reprimanded, but

Papa hadn't seemed really upset. It was her mother who was fussing about the new plastic jug. She supposed it was expensive.

Philippe entered the dining room holding something behind his back. His face wore a serious expression. Cora sat down and folded her hands in her lap. She bowed her head and closed her eyes to say grace.

"Bless us Oh Lord, and these thy gifts, which we are about to receive, from thy bounty, through Christ, Our Lord. Amen," the three said in unison.

Cora looked up to see her father smiling. An oblong canteen with a green canvas cover snapped around the body lay by her plate. There was a tiny chain to keep the lid from getting lost, and a sturdy belt made from webbing.

"For me, Papa?" Cora asked, her eyes shining.

"Yes, my little wild child. It was mine in the army, but I think you will get more use from it now."

"O boy! I can't wait to show Jimmie. Thank you, Papa. And Mom, you too. I'm really sorry about the Tupperware," Cora repeated. Her eyes filled with tears.

"We know you are, dear," Reeta said softly. "You have such interesting needs for a young girl."

7. RIIINNNG, RIIINNNG, RING

The next morning, Jimmie rushed through his chores. He did them all, but maybe not as carefully as some days. Then he ran to Laszlo Szep's house. Laszlo lived next door, across the creek and one field away. In fact, Jimmie's father owned the house Laszlo lived in. The Szeps were Hungarian tenant farmers, which meant they rented from the Moshers and also worked for them. They had come to the Mosher farm in the spring.

Laszlo was only a year younger than Jimmie, and they had become friends right away. Jimmie explained about the man named Veli who was sick and was staying in an old cabin on Fishkill Lake.

"He keeps talking some kind of gibberish. Maybe you can understand him," Jimmie said.

"Where is he from?" Laszlo asked.

"We don't know. He's so sick he only woke up for short times and asked for help. Maybe Veli will be better today."

"Veli Bej[4] is a famous bath in Budapest," Laszlo said.

"How can a bath be famous? You get wet, you soap up, rinse and dry off. What's the big deal?"

"These are hot springs that are supposed to make people well. People come from all over to soak."

"Wow," said Jimmie. "Maybe that's not the man's name. Maybe he wants to go to Hungary and take a bath."

"I don't think we could help him with that. It's a long trip," Laszlo said.

They asked for permission to phone Cora from Laszlo's house. They were all on the same party line and the call didn't have to go through an operator. Jimmie thought that was a good thing. Operators sometimes listened in on calls, even though they weren't supposed to.

---

[4] say VEL-ee bay

The phone was a big wooden box fastened to the wall. On the front was a conical mouthpiece with two bells above it. The left side of the box had a spring cradle that held an earpiece attached to the circuits inside the box by a cord. On the right was a crank. Each house on the same party line had a phone number that began with the same set of numbers and a letter. The Mosher, Szep and Dubois phone numbers all began with 43J. Jimmie's ended with 2, so his complete number was 43J2. If the phone bells made two long rings, everyone on the line could hear it, but they knew it was a call that should be picked up at the Mosher house.

Laszlo's number was more difficult. His was 43J23. That meant there were two long rings followed by three short rings And Cora's was 43J21. So two long rings followed by one short ring was a call for someone in the Dubois household. You were only supposed to pick up the phone if the call was meant for your house, but sometimes people would eavesdrop. This was very bad manners, but it happened a lot. Jimmie hoped no one would choose to listen to this conversation.

Calls to a different line had to go through an operator. This was a person who sat at a switchboard and plugged in the lines to send your call where you wanted it to go. First, you always had to check to see if someone else on the line was using the phone, so you would lift the earpiece and listen. If the line was clear you could hang up and make your call. To get the operator, you cranked the handle for one long ring. But for party line calls, you just cranked the code number, waited a few seconds and picked up the earpiece after you thought the other person had time to answer.

Jimmie was just barely tall enough to use the phone without standing on a stool. He let the cradle spring up by removing the earpiece and listened. No one else was on the line. He hung up and cranked the handle for two long rings and then one short one. A few seconds later he picked it up again. Cora's mother was saying, "Hello, hello."

"Mrs. Dubois, could I talk to Cora, please? This is Jimmie Mosher."

"Of course, Jimmie. I'll put her on the line."

There were sounds of muffled voices, and the scraping of a chair across the floor. The Dubois' phone was also mounted on the wall—too high for children to use comfortably.

Then Cora's voice came through the earpiece. "Hi, Jimmie."

"Hi, yourself. Laszlo's here with me. Can you talk?"

"Maybe."

"OK, I'll tell you stuff and you just answer. Laszlo hasn't got a bike, so we'll have to walk. That will take us maybe a half hour. I know how to get there without getting in the swamp now."

"That's great," Cora said.

"It's farther for you, but is that about how long it took you to ride home last night?"

"Yes."

"Do you have an extra lunch we can take to Veli?"

"No."

"OK, We'll try to get enough food at this end," Jimmie said.

"See you soon. I've got something special," Cora said. She hung up first.

"That was very mysterious," Cora's mother commented.

"Oh, I just want to show him my new canteen," Cora said.

8. IS HE HUNGARIAN?

It wasn't a problem to pack her own lunch, but after yesterday's raid on the pantry, Cora was afraid additional food would be missed. She did pack two bananas along with a peanut butter sandwich and a few cookies. Today she left her fragile, stinky thermos bottle home, and filled the wonderful canteen with cool clear water from the kitchen pump.

Jimmie and Laszlo also made sandwiches and then folded squares of wax paper neatly around them. Laszlo's mother said they could have four boiled eggs, a hunk of cheese, and some fresh cookies. "Thanks, Mrs. Szep," Jimmie said. "Next time we go out for the day we'll make the lunch at my house."

"Not to worry. We are neighbors," Maria Szep said in her broad Hungarian accent. "The eggs are gift from your chickens, anyway."

They tied all the food in a bandana and put it in a canvas rucksack. Jimmie filled his canteen, and Laszlo pumped water into a milk bottle and plugged the top with a big cork.

"That's not a good idea," Jimmie said. "It's glass."

"I'll just have to be careful. We don't have many extra things yet," Laszlo answered, tucking an old sweater around the bottle to protect it.

"Sorry," Jimmie said, "I forgot." He knew Laszlo was referring to his family's long, difficult trip from Hungary when they hardly had enough food to eat. They'd only had their clothes and a few possessions.

Laszlo put on the rucksack, and Jimmie carried the walking stick, prudently.

"You be good boys today," Mrs. Szep said.

"We will," they answered together, running out the door and heading across the road and into the woods.

They alternately jogged and walked, and reached the cabin ahead of Cora.

Jimmie sniffed the air and looked toward the stovepipe chimney. "No smoke. Veli hasn't lit the stove. Is he still sleeping?"

"Maybe he's gone," Laszlo said.

Leaves crunched behind them, and Cora arrived on her bike.

"What are you waiting for?" She asked, casually dismounting and adjusting the canteen belt. It was much too large for her waist, but she had strapped it diagonally across her chest.

"We just got here," Jimmie explained. "Hey, what's that?"

"My new canteen. It was my father's in the army."

"That's cool," Laszlo said. He sounded a little jealous.

The friends carefully navigated the rotting porch and pushed open the door. Veli lay beneath the blankets. He didn't appear to have moved since yesterday. But the cup Cora had filled with juice was empty, and the towel with a damp washcloth was hung over the bed frame.

"Is he dead?" Laszlo whispered.

Cora went and shook the man's shoulder. He groaned and rolled over to face her. His eyes tried to focus. Then, suddenly, he reached out with his other hand and grabbed Cora by the arm! More of the strange sounds poured from his mouth. There was no way to understand what the man had in mind.

"Hey!" Jimmie yelled. "What are you doing? Don't you hurt her. There are two more of us and I have a weapon." He raised the walking stick like a baseball bat.

The man cringed, and his eyes rolled wildly. He released his hold on Cora and fell back into the leaf-filled pillowcase.

"He's still awfully hot and feverish," Cora said. "If he doesn't get better soon, we'll have to get a doctor whether he wants it or not. Veli wasn't trying to hurt me, I'm pretty certain. But he sure wants to tell us something."

Veli continued to mumble, and Laszlo was listening. "Whatever he's trying to say, it's not in Hungarian. Or German, either, I'm pretty sure. I heard that a lot when I was little. But I don't speak any German."

"Now what do we do?" Jimmie asked, looking at the man who was again unconscious.

"The same as we did yesterday." Cora said. "We take care of him till he gets better or we decide we need help."

She handed the bucket to Laszlo. "More clean water, so I can cool him down," she demanded.

"I'll build up the fire," Jimmie said. "He'll need more tea."

"Yes, and use your can opener on that applesauce. We forgot he couldn't open it even if he wanted to. I'll poach an egg and mash a banana, too. He's weak from not eating."

The three friends worked hard for the next few hours, although it didn't feel the same as doing chores, since it was something out of the ordinary. Their hope was that Veli would get better, and that they could figure out what was bothering him so much. Cora bathed the man's face and neck, and fed him small portions of food whenever he woke. The boys collected firewood and heated an entire bucket of water on the stove.

They washed the man's shirt, which smelled of sour sweat, and hung it outside to dry in the sun. They cleaned the windows and even scrubbed the outhouse. With the twine they lashed a brace on the table leg. Cora had brought an old tablecloth. The cabin was never going to be livable without major repairs, but at mid-day it looked like a completely different place from when Jimmie first found the man.

It was too warm inside, and there was only the one chair, so the friends sat on the edge of the porch to eat their own lunches.

Cora heard Veli groan. "I have to check on him," she said.

They went back inside just in time to see him sit up and twist to rest his feet on the floor. His gaze roamed around the room and across their faces. But his eyes no longer looked bright and wild.

"The fever's broken," Cora said.

"Where am I?" Veli asked. "And who are you children?"

9. VELI TELLS HIS STORY

Cora was astonished. "You know me! We gave you a ride on Sunday. It was only a few days ago."

"You are that little girl?" The man was speaking with an accent, but he was using English, and they could understand him well enough.

"My name is Cora. I told you that yesterday, and you told us your name is Veli. Is that true?"

"Yes, yes it is. I don't remember much since... But who are these boys?"

"I'm Jimmie. I was exploring and found you here in bed. I brought Cora, and our friend Laszlo came to help, too. He speaks Hungarian, but he couldn't understand you."

"And this is my cabin? It was dirty and cold. Everything smelled bad. I don't understand. What day is this?" Veli looked confused.

"Wednesday," Cora explained. "We cleaned. Things have to be clean for sick people to get well."

"Thank you, kind children. Perhaps you can help me in another way, as well."

Cora was suddenly suspicious. "Are you a spy?"

"A spy! Why would you think that?" Veli asked. "I am just an old man searching for someone."

Cora was glad he wasn't a spy, although that had sounded very exciting. And she wondered if a spy would admit he was one. So maybe she shouldn't believe him. But maybe his story would be interesting in a different way.

"Oh, I was just pretending. Who are you looking for?" she asked. "Wait. You need food and water first. We have boiled eggs and I can make oatmeal. Those will be good for you."

So, Veli's tale had to wait a little longer while he visited the outhouse, and food and tea were prepared. Jimmie and Laszlo filled the pillowcase with fresh leaves, as the old ones had broken down and were no longer comfortable.

Finally, the man sat on the bed, leaning against the wall with the pillow at his back, and the children arranged themselves in front of him, sitting on the floor with crossed legs. Veli held a fresh cup of tea in his hands. He took a sip and began.

"I am a Finn."

Cora gasped. "So is my mother, but we didn't know or she could have translated. She doesn't speak any Finnish at home."

"It does not matter. I will use English now. I'm sorry if I frightened you."

"It's OK, you were really sick," Jimmie said.

"If we can keep my secret a little longer, I would be very grateful." Veli said.

Laszlo was wary. "Secrets aren't good, sometimes. We had to run away from Hungary because the government wanted to keep it a secret that they were treating people badly."

"I understand," Veli said. "I can see that you are wise beyond your years. Mine is not a bad kind of secret."

"We'll listen, and help you if it won't get us in trouble," Cora said. "We already had to sneak food out of our houses, and although we didn't lie, it doesn't feel right. My mom suspects something is going on."

Veli leaned forward and placed the empty cup on the floor. Then he sat back and sighed. "I have a granddaughter I have never met. I don't even know her name. I think she is a little older than any of you."

"Golly," Jimmie said, "How could you not know her name?"

"Her mother is my daughter. We had a fight many years ago, and she left home. She said she would never speak to me again. And she has kept her promise."

"But why are you looking for her here," Laszlo asked.

"A friend of hers has kept in touch. This person told me she married, had a baby girl and moved to Cherry Hill. But I don't know her new last name. My daughter's name is Oona. Do you know a woman with that name?"

Jimmie, Laszlo and Cora looked at each other and all shook their heads. "Jimmie and Laszlo have only lived here a few months. But I never heard of anyone with that name," Cora said.

"It means 'one,'" Veli said. "She was our only child, we knew we could not have any others."

"Cora and I are only children too. But Laszlo has two sisters," Jimmie said.

"Margit is older, and Eniko is little yet," Laszlo explained.

Veli nodded. "Now my wife has died. I am getting old, and I would like to give her locket to my granddaughter before I, too, pass away. Maybe she would like to meet her old grandfather."

Perhaps he wasn't tactful, but Laszlo was honest. "We thought you were dead when we came this morning. You were so still."

"I thank you again for helping me to get well. This makes me wish to find the girl as soon as possible. Next time, I might not have such good helpers as you have been." He paused and pointed to the valise. "Please bring me my bag."

Laszlo jumped up and lifted the brown leather bag onto the bed beside Veli. The man rummaged around inside until he brought out a small box, the kind of box you would see at a jewelry store, with a red velvet cover and a hinged lid. He opened it.

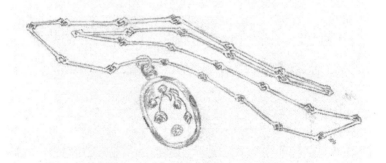

With his thin and rough fingers he carefully lifted a gold locket from the box. It was oval and fastened to a beautiful chain with links like thin bars with little interlocked rings at the ends. He beckoned to Cora.

"Will you open it for me? My old fingers are so stiff."

Cora stood and reached for the precious ornament. She slipped a fingernail into the catch and snapped it open. On the left was a picture of a smiling couple.

"That is me with my wife Sonja when we were young," Veli pointed to the picture and explained. "And over here on the right is Oona as a young girl."

The boys also came closer to look at the pictures.

"We'll try to help you," Jimmie said. "But why keep it a secret? I'll bet one of our parents will know your daughter."

"And then they will tell. They will talk to her and Oona will send me away without letting me speak to the child." Veli sounded anxious, and he grabbed a bed post for support. "I'm very tired now, children. I need to sleep more. Can you come again?"

"We'll try," Cora said.

Veli reached in his valise and pulled out a battered wallet. He gave Jimmie some money. "You are the oldest, correct?"

"Yes, Jimmie answered.

"You can buy some food for me, please. Then you will not have to steal at home. Maybe some sardines." Veli stretched out on the bed. He was exhausted.

"Sure thing," Jimmie said. But he wasn't at all sure about getting to town without a parent's help.

11. CHERRY HILL COURTHOUSE

The next day, Jimmie and Laszlo had to help pick and sort sweet cherries all day long. They talked on the phone with Cora, and she said she would ride her bike to the cabin to check on Veli and take him a little more food.

That evening, the boys sat in the hideout they'd discovered several weeks ago[5] discussing the problem. They needed to buy groceries. There was a tiny store at Cherry Pit Junction. They could ride their bikes there, but the food was expensive and most of the customers were people who worked at the canning factory who bought things for their lunches. There were sure to be questions that would get back to Cora's father.

Surprisingly, the solution came from Mr. Szep. There was a knock on the doorframe and

---

[5] see The Secret Cellar, Dubois Files #1

Laszlo's dad poked his head inside. "You boys want earn spare change tomorrow?" he asked.

"Wow!" Laszlo said.

"Yes!" Jimmie said.

"You take cherries to town with me. I pay you to load and unload truck at grocery. Mr. Volger give me good money."

Jimmie immediately asked, "Can Cora come too? You don't have to pay any extra. But she's our friend."

"Sure, sure," Istvan Szep said. "Lots of room for good children. Eight-thirty sharp, though."

"I'll telephone and see if she can come," Jimmie said.

The boys punched each other as a goodbye and headed to their homes.

***

After unloading the cherries and receiving ten cents each for their work, Istvan said, "I go do errands. Buy chicken feed. Buy nails. You come hardware store at noon, or you are walking home." He chuckled.

"We'll be there," Cora said.

With thirty cents to spend, the friends went inside the grocery store. After buying Tootsie Rolls, atomic fireball Jaw Breakers and a big Sugar Daddy lollipop to share they still had fifteen cents.

When they were sure Mr. Szep had driven away, they bought tins of sardines, canned milk, oatmeal, cheese, bread and more tea bags for Veli. They spent all the money he had given them plus three cents of their own money. The groceries filled the rucksack they'd brought. And it was heavy. Mr. Volger gave them a long look as they checked out, but he didn't ask any questions.

"Now the courthouse," Cora said.

"Why?" the boys asked.

"To check public records. Maybe we can find out who Oona married," Cora explained.

The courthouse was two blocks away. It was an imposing building of gray stone that made the children feel that life was serious. Jimmie shouldered the heavy pack and they walked across the park eating their candy as they went.

"We should have left these groceries in the back of the truck somehow," Jimmie said. "The bread's getting smashed and the straps hurt."

"I'll take a turn," Laszlo said. "After we're done at the courthouse."

"Let's hide it in the bushes while we're inside. Too many questions from adults," Cora said.

"Good idea," Jimmie agreed.

They quenched their thirst after the sweets at the drinking fountain in the park.

The courthouse was gloomy inside, with closed doors on each side of the huge hallway. The doors had labels like "County Prosecutor," "Treasurer," "Clerk," and "Registrar of Deeds."

"Wow, which office do we need?" Laszlo asked. He felt very small.

A woman was walking toward them.

"Where do we find out about marriage licenses?" Cora asked her.

"Aren't you a little young?" the woman said, laughing at her own joke.

Jimmie got red. "Not for us," he said. "We need to find out who someone married."

The woman smiled and put her finger to her lips. "I won't tell." Apparently she still thought they were cute children playing a game. "County Clerk's office. Right there." She pointed at one of the doors.

"Thank you," Cora said politely, but she was fuming over not being taken seriously.

The counter in the Clerk's office was too high for the children. Laszlo could barely see over it, and Jimmie and Cora were only an inch or so taller. Nevertheless, the lady who waited on them was polite, not like the woman in the hall.

"We need to find a marriage record," Cora began. "A woman named Oona who got married about fifteen years ago."

The woman had seemed willing to help them, but now she said, "I'm not sure I can do that."

Jimmie was irked. He didn't like being treated as a child. "Because we aren't grownups?" He asked. "Or does it cost money?" He dug in a pocket and pulled out six cents, which he placed on the counter.

The others reached for their remaining change, and the total they had left was twelve cents.

"It's not the money, although if you want a certified copy of a marriage record it will cost a nickel," the woman asked.

"So it is because we are kids," Cora said, also feeling quite put out.

"Not at all," the woman said. "As far as I know, there's no age requirement to make a request, although it's a little unusual."

"Then what?" Laszlo asked. "We are trying to be polite."

"Oh dear. I thought you would understand. The records are filed by last name and cross referenced for both the husband and the wife's maiden name. You'll need a last name to find this couple. And 'Oona' is quite common around here. So many Finns, you know."

The boys turned to leave.

But Cora had another thought. "What about births?" she asked.

"Same situation, Miss. We need a last name."

"Thank you, anyway," Cora said.

11. DELIVERING THE GROCERIES

Cora, Jimmie and Laszlo sat on kegs in their hideout eating peanut butter sandwiches.

"We've got to get this pack of food to Veli and find out his last name," Jimmie said between bites.

"I can't believe we didn't think to ask him," Cora said in disgust. "Maybe he is a spy, or he would have told us. And how did he know about that cabin?"

Jimmie swiped at Cora in a mock slap. "You're obsessed with spies."

Cora ducked, but she grinned.

"Well, at least we got the groceries in here without my dad seeing them," Laszlo said.

Cora was still glum. "Doggone it. I have to go home and help can cherries. Mom let me come with you this morning, but I've been out a lot this week."

"Hey, let me go get the phone book," Jimmie said suddenly. He jumped up and ran out the door.

In a minute he was back with the slim paper directory of Cherry Hill, Thorpe and Cherry Pit Junction telephone numbers.

"Let's look for anyone named Oona," he said.

It was too dark in the hideout to read the fine print, so they went outside and sprawled in the grass. After scanning just a few pages, Cora said, "This is no good. Only the husband's names are printed, except for some old ladies who aren't married, or they're widows."

"Well, it was worth a try," Jimmie said. He sounded a little defensive.

"I have to go," Cora said. "Call me tonight." She stood, retrieved her bike from where it lay in the grass, and pedaled away.

***

Actually, Cora called Jimmie. She cranked out the two long rings and waited till Jimmie was put on the line after his mother answered. Children did not answer the telephone.

"We canned fourteen quarts of cherries and made a batch of jam," she said. "I'm beat. But Mom says I can play tomorrow because I was such a big help."

"Hot dog! But Laszlo has to help move hay and repair the fences."

"Oh. Jimmie, you can't carry that heavy pack to the cabin all alone. I'll ride over and we'll hike in together," Cora offered.

"Thanks."

"I'll come over right after breakfast."

"OK, I'll be hoeing the garden. The weeds are growing like crazy. But I'll work fast."

***

Cora arrived in the morning bringing a canvas tote bag. It wasn't as good as the rucksack for carrying things, which you could put on your back, but it was better than the pillowcase had been.

They split the provisions between the pack and the tote, took their full canteens and two sticks from the workshop, and set out to hike to the cabin by the lake. They had gone only a short distance when Cora set down the tote bag and said, "I have an idea."

"What?" asked Jimmie.

Cora took off the canteen belt and slipped her slender arm through the handles of the tote bag, pushing the bag up to her shoulder. "Now help me fasten that belt through the straps and around under my other arm," she said.

Jimmie complied. "How's that?"

It wasn't very comfortable, but it did free up her hands. "Not great, but at least it's not pulling my arm out of joint," Cora said.

They reached the cabin and Veli was excited to see them. "I thought maybe you abandoned me," he said. But there was a twinkle in his eye.

"We couldn't get away yesterday. If you don't want our parents to know about you, we can't just tell them why we disappear for so long," Jimmie said.

"But we did manage to get you all this food without having to explain," Cora added, releasing the canteen belt. The bag of groceries thumped onto the floor. "I hope you didn't go hungry waiting for us."

"I caught a fish in the lake," Veli said. "I have some line and a hook or two in my bag."

Jimmie and Cora explained to Veli that they had tried to find Oona by getting public records at the courthouse, but he hadn't told them any last names.

"My last name is Seppanen," Veli said. "I forgot to tell you. I was not quite well the other day. Now I am much better. But I don't know the name of the man she married."

"I'm glad you're better," Cora said, giving Veli a little hug. "I think you took a bath, too."

"Yes, young lady, I did. You cleaned my old house up so nice, I thought I should be clean too."

"Your old house? We didn't know that," Jimmie exclaimed.

"Yes, when I first came to this country, many years ago, I bought the land and built this little home here on Fishkill Lake. But when I married my Sonja, it was too small. We moved away."

Just then, a crack of thunder sounded outside the windows. None of them had noticed how dark the sky had become.

"Jeepers creepers," Jimmie said, we'd better head for home, quick."

12. THE STORM

The children dumped the contents of their bags on the floor, grabbed the walking sticks and headed outside.

The clouds overhead were dark purple and ominous. A blackish mass swallowed the sun and the woods became almost as dark as night.

"We're all right," Jimmie said. "I know the way really well, but we have to hurry or we'll get soaked."

They ran as fast as they could, but in just a few minutes a gust of wind blew leaves and even small twigs off the trees, and then large drops of water began to pelt down on their heads and arms. Neither had thought to bring a jacket. It was a warm morning when they had left home. In only a few more minutes, their clothes were wet through.

"I'm getting cold," Cora said.

"Me too. We have to keep moving. It we stop we'll get too cold."

But in the rush to get home, and with the sun covered by dark clouds, Jimmie hadn't been keeping a careful eye on where he was. The wind made the tree limbs dance wildly, confusing everything. They were running, squinting with the rain in their faces. All of a sudden, Jimmie found himself in water that was almost up to his waist.

Cora jumped backwards to avoid falling in herself. Not only was the water deep but it was moving swiftly.

"I need help! I can't keep my feet under me," Jimmie yelled. He was grabbing at the weeds which were bending in the current, and trying to use his own stick to steady himself.

Cora lay down on the solid ground where she was and extended her stick till Jimmie caught hold of it. "Now I'll back up and you try to come toward me."

He half-swam and pushed with his feet. Soon he was lying safe beside his friend, and panting hard. "That was close," he said. "I guess I can't get any wetter than this."

"Where are we?" Cora asked. "Did we get turned around and end up at the lake?"

"I don't think so. The rain came down so hard that the swamp overflowed. I bet the creek is flooded, too. Maybe even over the road." His teeth were chattering.

"Jimmie, your lips are blue. I'm really cold too. Can we get back to the cabin?"

"I think so," Jimmie said.

The two friends held hands and began to retrace their steps. The sky was darker than ever, and when a bolt of lightning lit up the woods it hurt their eyes. The thunder that followed wasn't as dangerous, but it sounded menacing.

"I don't think you're supposed to be under trees in a thunderstorm," Cora said.

"Not under one tree, because lightning might strike it. Maybe a whole forest full is safer," Jimmie replied. "We haven't got much choice anyway. Boy, everything sure looks different in this weird light."

"There's the real lake." Cora pointed ahead and to the left.

"Horray! That means we'll find the cabin soon."

But just then, the wind gusted, howling between the trunks of the trees, and with a great crashing sound a heavy limb fell, missing them by inches. One of the smaller branches caught in the strap of Cora's overalls and pulled her to the ground.

"Cora, are you hurt?" Jimmie shouted, trying to make himself heard above the noise of the wind.

"I'm OK, but my pants are caught. Help me get loose."

Cora couldn't reach the buckle, but Jimmie got to it, and slipped the strap free from the button. Then he used his stick as a pry bar to bend the branch away from Cora.

"Close your eyes, so you don't get poked," he yelled.

Cora did, and then she squirmed out from under the fallen limb. She wiggled her arms and legs to be sure everything worked all right, and fastened her overall strap.

"Jimmie, do you smell smoke?"

"Yes! Veli must have built a fire. It's over that way. Let's go."

Since Veli had no lantern or candle there wasn't a light to guide them in, but Jimmie had a good nose, and they were soon standing inside the single room of the cabin, dripping on the floor. Water ran from a few leaks in the roof, creating puddles.

"The creek is flooded, and we couldn't make it home," Jimmie said.

Cora added, "It's a good thing you lit the stove. We could smell the smoke and found the way back by it."

"You children are soaked to the skin," Veli said. You'd better get out of those wet clothes and sit by the stove. You can wrap up in my blankets."

13. RESCUE

Jimmie and Cora took turns getting undressed while Veli held the sheet to make a changing room. They sat by the stove, Cora wrapped in the crocheted afghan and Jimmie in the brown plaid wool.

Veli now had the pleasure of waiting on them. He heated water and made hot tea, although they had to share the one cup. He took their clothes to the porch and wrung them out till they were no longer dripping. Then he spread them over the back of the chair and on the table, near the stove, to dry.

The worst of the storm passed, and the rain was no longer coming down as hard, but the sky remained dark. It felt like evening instead of mid-afternoon.

Jimmie and Cora stopped shaking as they warmed up, and soon felt quite comfortable. But their clothes were still damp.

Outside, a growling noise approached through the trees. Twin beams of light shot through the front window of the cabin. Both children jumped up to look outside.

"It's my dad's car!" Cora said, astonished. "How did he know we were here?"

"It doesn't matter," said Jimmie. "Put your clothes on quick. I won't look. Push all that food under the bed or something. Let's hope he doesn't come inside because there's no back door where Veli can sneak out."

Cora struggled into her damp shirt and overalls, but the bib and buckles made it difficult. Jimmie managed to get dressed first, and ran outside onto the porch.

Veli began collecting anything that might give away his presence—clothing, his shaving mug, and mirror. He stuffed them into the old valise, and pushed it far under the bed. He covered the bed with the brown blanket, because it hung down enough to hide things underneath.

Cora's father was just getting out of the car. He left the motor running and the headlights on.

"Wow! Mr. Dubois, are we glad to see you!" Jimmie said.

"You gave us quite a scare young man. Where's Cora?"

Just then, his daughter came through the front door, and ran to her father's arms. "Oh, Papa, we're fine. We just got caught in the storm, and the creek was flooded, and we got all wet so we came back to the cabin to light a fire in the stove and dry off. We didn't mean to worry you."

"Whose house is this?" Philippe Dubois asked.

"It's just an old empty cabin, sir," Jimmie said. "We've sort of been playing house this week."

"And you have a fire going?"

"Yes," Jimmie said slowly. He was afraid he was going to be in trouble. Maybe Mr. Dubois didn't think he was old enough to light a fire. "I checked the stovepipe and didn't do anything foolish. I know how. It's just like the one in my dad's workshop."

"Your parents called when you two weren't home before the storm. Jed thought you'd been playing near the lake. Your mother was very worried."

Jimmie hung his head. "I'm sorry. It's my fault. I should have paid more attention to the sky. But we started for home as soon as we noticed. Then the path was under water, and a tree fell right in front of us, so we knew we'd be safer here."

Philippe nodded. "That makes a lot of sense. Let's see this cabin of yours."

"It's nothing much, Papa."

"No matter, let's see where you've been hiding out."

Reluctantly, the children led the way toward the cabin.

"Watch your step. The porch floor is pretty bad," Jimmie said. Maybe he spoke a little louder than was necessary.

Cora pushed open the door and stood inside holding the knob. Veli was nowhere in sight, and there was no evidence that anyone other than the children had been there, except the brown plaid blanket. Cora hoped her father would assume it had come from Jimmie's house.

Philippe Dubois stood in the doorway and took in the mended table leg, the tablecloth and cup with used tea bags lying in the dish. He saw the stove and felt the warmth it gave to the room, despite the two spots where water still dripped through the roof. The bed was made with the afghan he recognized and another blanket. There were two eggs on one of the shelves.

"You haven't been sleeping here?" he asked.

"No, of course not, but there's only one chair, so we just pretended the bed was a couch," Cora said.

"You kept your heads, came back to shelter, built a fire, dried out, and made hot drinks all on your own," it wasn't a question, but a statement.

"Yes, Papa. We aren't little children any more," Cora said.

"I can see that. Well, James Mosher, I think we should take you home and tell your parents what a fine job you've done taking care of my daughter."

Jimmie stood up tall. "Thank you, but Cora saved my life. I slipped into the creek and she pulled me out. Then I got her untangled from the tree. We both did fine jobs today. We're sorry to have worried everyone, but we would have come right home as soon as it was safe."

"You are right. It's a new world, and girls, especially one little girl I know," he nodded at Cora, "are extremely capable. Now, let's get you two home."

Philippe headed for the car. As soon as his back was turned, Cora ducked behind the door and gave Veli a quick hug, then ran to follow her father. Jimmie lingered just long enough to shake their friend's hand, then grabbed the canteens and walking sticks, pulled the door shut and sprinted for the car.

14. WHO IS OONA?

Now that part of their secret was out, Jimmie, Cora and Laszlo were afraid they would be barred from visiting the cabin. They were relieved when Jed Mosher said thoughtfully, "There was a hermit of some sort who lived there when I was a child. He's been gone for years. I guess you aren't hurting anything to play there. I'd warn you not to do anything dangerous, but you've been quite responsible lately, Jimmie. I'm proud of you."

"That was a close one," Lazlo said, in response to the story of the storm, as told to him by Jimmie and Cora. They were eating cookies in the cellar hideout.

"In more ways than one," Jimmie agreed.

Cora burst out laughing. "A hermit! That had to be Veli. He would have been already grown up when your dad was a kid."

"So, now we know their last name is Seppanen, but when can we get back to the courthouse to find out who Oona married?" Jimmie asked. My folks went shopping today, but the courthouse is closed on Saturday so I stayed here.

Laszlo kicked restlessly at an empty keg. "I don't know when Apa will go to town again. He took the rest of the sweet cherries, the ones that weren't as perfect, to the canning factory to be made into juice."

"Do we have to keep taking food to Veli?" Cora asked. "He's well now. Maybe he can go buy his own food."

"He's got plenty for a few days, anyway," Jimmie said. "Maybe I can check on him tomorrow after church. He might not be quite strong enough to walk to town yet."

"Wow, it was only a week ago that I met him," Cora said, shaking her head.

Jimmie changed the subject. "We've got to get a bike for Laszlo. Then we could all ride to town. It's five miles, but we can take the back road and be safer than on Centerline and the Highway."

"Don't forget, I have to ride almost three miles just to get here, first," Cora complained.

"Yeah, but you're tough for a girl." Jimmie looked at his friend and grinned.

***

The following day was Sunday, but there were no long car trips planned by the Dubois family. Cora was glad. After church was over and dinner was eaten, she changed into her favorite overalls and got out the notebook in which she recorded interesting things she found.

Usually, on Sunday afternoon, her parents took naps. Cora couldn't understand how people got tired in the middle of the day. But the house was quiet, and she knew she wouldn't be disturbed.

She had not yet had time to study the old newspaper from the cabin that they hadn't needed to burn. Now, she spread the pieces out on a table in her bedroom that also served as a desk.

She could see, at the top of the pages, the name Cherry Hill Herald. So this was the local paper. The date was October 9, 1918. She didn't have the front page, only parts of some interior ones. Even so, it was easy to get a sense of the news. She carefully wrote on a clean sheet in her notebook the date she found the papers, the date the paper was published, and all the headlines and stories on the pages she had.

There was a continuation of a story about a World War I battle in France where a man named Alvin York killed twenty-five Germans and took 132 prisoners all by himself. There was an ad for Coca-Cola (at least I've heard of that, she thought), and the movie "The Great Dictator" starring Charlie Chaplin, was playing at the Starlight Theater. There was social news about a dinner party at the home of some people Cora had never heard of, and also a listing of births and deaths.

Suddenly, she had an idea. She just had to wait for her mother to wake up. She spent the rest of the nap time making lists in her notebook of the articles in the old newspaper.

In about an hour, she heard dishes rattling in the kitchen, and she ran down the stairs.

"Mom, I found a funny name in an old newspaper that was at the cabin we were playing in."

"What name is that, dear?" Reeta Dubois asked.

Cora opened her notebook to the place where she had added an item that wasn't really in the paper. She had written "Oona Seppanen, born to Veli and Sonja Seppanen." She knew the year was wrong; Oona wasn't born until after Veli moved away, but it had to be close. And she knew her own mother was Finnish.

"Is Oona a name for a girl or a boy?" she asked

"It's a girl's name. It's Finnish. Actually, there are several women named Oona in Forest County. Many Finns settled here."

Her mother looked at the notebook where Cora was pointing.

"Seppanen. That just means "smith."

"Like a blacksmith or a silversmith?" Cora asked.

"Exactly like that. Veli means "brother" and Sonja is "wise."

"So the father is really just Brother Smith. That doesn't sound as interesting. What does Oona mean?" Of course Cora already knew the answer to this question, but she couldn't tell her mother that.

"One. Perhaps she was their first child. Why does this interest you, Cora?"

"Maybe if she still lives here I could interview her. We're sure to have to write an essay about summer vacation when school starts."

"Helping to save the Mosher farm and being caught in that big storm aren't enough for you? Heavens to Betsy, child!"

"But does she live here?" Cora persisted.

"I believe so. I think she's married to Ralph Ramsey."

15. CHERRY SOUP

The next day, Jimmie and Laszlo had to help on the farm by sorting tart cherries. A couple of boards were laid across two sawhorses in Jimmie's yard, to make a long narrow table. Big pails of cherries had been brought from the orchard and the children were dividing them into clean containers. The best ones would be taken to Volger's Grocery store. Mr. Volger would buy them outright, or trade for groceries if the farmers preferred that. He would re-sell them in his produce department. Second best would be sold to the canning factory. Of course, the Moshers kept some for their own use.

Cora wasn't required to help with this job, but it gave her the opportunity to visit, and it was likely she'd be given some cherries to take home to her family.

"Do you really think you can get away with that school essay idea?" Jimmie asked Cora.

"Why not? It might be a great story. I can ask Oona what she remembers about growing up here."

"Yeah, but you didn't really see her name in the paper, and we need her daughter, not her. We don't even know the girl's name yet," Laszlo pointed out.

"Do you have a better idea?" Cora thought the boys shouldn't be able to tell her how to follow up on her plan.

She popped a cherry in her mouth. It was refreshing, but sour. These cherries weren't sweet like the earlier varieties, but they made the best pies. She spit out the pit.

"Someone will tell us Veli's granddaughter's name, now that we know who her dad is. Then just call her on the phone," Laszlo suggested.

Cora snorted. "And out of nowhere tell her we know her grandfather, someone she's never met, and he wants to give her a gift? Maybe Oona told her he's dead, or that he hates them. We know Oona doesn't want to talk to Veli. Besides, the operator might be listening. 'Don't tell secrets over the phone,' my mother says."

"But we should be able to find out the girl's name without making anyone suspicious," Jimmie said.

"Margit will be in eighth grade this fall," Laszlo said, referring to his older sister. "This girl might be in the same grade. At least she's in the same school."

"Can we trust Margit not to spill the beans?" Jimmie asked. He threw a handful of wormy cherries in a bucket that would go to the chickens.

"We don't have to tell her the whole story. Just say that we were curious about Finnish families in Cherry Hill," Laszlo said.

"That sounds really fishy," Cora said. "I think we have to try to make friends with this girl, so she isn't suspicious. She might think we're being too nosy."

"This is getting complicated. And won't she be suspicious anyway if we just suddenly want to be her friend?" Laszlo asked.

Jimmie had been thinking. "I did look up the Ramseys in the phone book. They live right in town, on Birch Street. So she might not even want to talk to us farm kids."

Cora was getting impatient. "I think we have to ask Margit if she knows her. She can't make us tell her more if we don't want to, and it's no crime to just ask someone's name."

"We've been sorting cherries all morning," Laszlo said. "I'm hot. Let's find Margit and get something cold to drink."

The three dipped their sticky hands in a bucket of clean water and wiped them on an old towel kept nearby for that purpose. Then they raced to the Szep house.

Margit and her mother, Maria, were in the kitchen.

"Come in, now. You work so hard," Mrs. Szep said. "Have some cold cherry soup."

"Cherry soup!" Jimmie exclaimed. "I never heard of it."[6]

Margit smiled. "You'll like it. It's Hungarian. Tart cherries with spices and fresh yogurt."

Margit was right, the cherry soup was delicious.

---

[6] see Cherry soup recipe at the end of the book

16. CHURCH PICNIC

As it turned out, Margit wasn't even curious about why they wanted to know the Ramsey girl's name. "It's Beth," she said. "She's OK, she'll be in ninth grade this year. I think she's shy."

"So are you," Laszlo said bluntly. "You don't have any friends. I'll bet you're even too scared to invite her to the church picnic."

Margit gave Laszlo an intense stare. She picked up the phone book, thumbed it open and ran her finger down a page. She went to the telephone and turned the crank once for the operator, then picked up the earpiece. "Sixteen-R-three, please," she said when the operator answered.

Jimmie stared in awe at what Laszlo had set in motion.

"Could I speak to Beth? This is Margit Szep. I know her from school. Please."

Cora shook her head in wonder.

"Beth? This is Margit. There's a big picnic at my church this coming Sunday afternoon, and if you want to come you could sit with my family. We'll have plenty of food. It starts at one. It would be nice to have someone my own age to talk to. There are games and stuff, but most of them are for little kids."

She glared at Laszlo and stuck out her tongue.

"Do you want us to pick you up? OK. See you there. Bye."

"Yippie!" Laszlo yelled, as soon as his sister hung up.

"Don't think you're so smart," Margit said. "I get a prize in Sunday School for bringing a friend. I was going to invite someone. You just gave me the idea for who it should be. She said she'd walk and meet us there."

***

Sunday's church picnic was going to be a perfect opportunity to get acquainted with Beth and maybe tell her about her grandfather, but it was six days away.

In the meantime, Veli was going to need more food. Jimmie said he'd check on their friend.

Tuesday morning, he worked as fast, but carefully, as he could, and got so many cherries sorted that his father told him to go play for the afternoon. Laszlo, however, was stuck picking more cherries, so Jimmie was on his own.

In order to save time, he rode his bike directly to the small store at Cherry Pit Junction. He used his own money to buy a loaf of bread and some summer sausage. He'd thought about this for a long time, and thought that would be an ordinary kind of purchase that wouldn't cause anyone to question why he was buying groceries.

Then he pedaled back home and ran almost all the way to the cabin. Except for grumbling a little about not having any coffee for over a week, Veli was fine. He had caught more fish, and with the bread and sausage he now had plenty of food for the rest of the week. He paid Jimmie for the supplies.

Jimmie told him his granddaughter's name was Beth Ramsey and also about their plan to meet with her on Sunday.

Veli became excited. "Why don't I come to your picnic too? I can see the girl, but she won't know who I am, and then I can know her reaction."

Jimmie wasn't sure this was a good idea. "What if somebody recognizes you?"

"No one here has seen me for fifteen years. Your own father won't know who I am."

"My father? Why would he know you?" Jimmie asked. "How do you know my last name?"

"Cora's father called you Jimmie Mosher. Jed Mosher was a boy when I lived here. You look just the same as he did. That dark hair and eyes, with the pale face. You must be his son. Your grandfather was a good man, too."

Jimmie ducked his head. "He died. That's why we live on the farm now. Granny May is still alive, but she's getting funny in the head."

"It's too bad, boy. Too bad. We all get old."

"You'd need clean clothes for the picnic, or you'll stand out." Jimmie was worried that he and his friends would be in trouble for making friends with a hobo.

"Maybe that little girl could iron my shirt. Could you take it to her?"

"Cora? Maybe. But your suit is all wrinkled too."

"I have another pair of pants that aren't so worn. But only the one white shirt," Veli said.

He took it off and held it out to the boy with such a sad look in his eyes that Jimmie said, "OK, sure."

***

On Wednesday, Jimmie washed the shirt while his mother was busy doing something else, and hung it behind his own clothes to dry.

That evening, he delivered it to Cora. He'd called her and they met at the Thorpe River bridge, so no adult would see the shirt being transferred.

"I'll get it ironed somehow, and take it to Veli before Sunday," she promised. "How will he get to the picnic?"

"I guess he's going to walk," Jimmie said.

"Or thumb a ride," Cora added.

***

Sunday, by one o'clock families had begun to gather on the church lawn. Cora's family attended the Catholic church, but after that service, they walked to the Swedish Baptist Church to enjoy the picnic. The Moshers had invited them, knowing what good friends the children were.

Blankets were spread on the grass, and some people had brought lawn chairs. Long tables had been carried outside and placed end to end.

Everyone placed casserole dishes, or a salad or dessert on them as they arrived.

Two men exited the church carrying a huge soup pot that was filled instead with ice cold lemonade. A little girl trailed behind them holding two ladles. After the pot was safely placed on a table, the pastor banged on the side of the pot with one of the ladles and everyone quieted down while he gave thanks for the food.

After that, there was a huge rush to get in line for the feast. Margit and Beth were trying to act grown up, not running to be first like most of the kids. Cora joined them, and asked Margit who her friend was.

But Jimmie hung back, watching. He saw Veli come around the corner and step onto the church lawn.

17. LURE OF THE LOCKET

The girls had reached the tables and were filling their paper plates with mounds of chicken salad, baked beans and other delicious foods. The three of them acted as if they'd been lifelong friends, Jimmie thought, although Cora and Beth had met only minutes before. Their heads were close together and they were giggling and laughing. They took their plates to a blanket in the shade of a large tree and sat down to eat.

Veli also joined the line for food. The fact that he was all alone made it look like he was a bum who had wandered in for the free food, but so far, no one seemed to be paying any attention to him. That was a good thing, Jimmie thought. Making a scene would not help anyone. At least he was neat, wearing the clean, pressed shirt and a pair of gray trousers. That was good.

Jimmie decided to stay far away from Veli. He was afraid one of them might accidentally do something that would indicate they knew each other, so he waited until nearly everyone had filled their plates. Just as he got in line, Cora came up behind him and said, "I'm getting dessert already. You're just starting?"

"Yeah. Did you see our friend?" He asked.

"Yes. He looks pretty good, but I can't call him The Spy in Brown any more."

"But, he is kind of like a spy today," Jimmie chuckled. "He's probably figured out that one of the girls you're with is his granddaughter. He's watching you."

Cora dropped her voice to a whisper. "I'm going to try to get Beth to come over by my dad's car. I'll tell her I want to show her something."

"Show her what?"

"That's where you come in. Get the locket from Veli and meet us by the car in about five minutes."

"What if he doesn't have it with him? How am I supposed talk with him if I'm not supposed to know him?"

"Figure something out. Take him a piece of cake. He better have that locket!" she whispered fiercely.

Jimmie balanced his own plate along with two small plates of cake and walked toward the tree where Veli was seated with his back against the trunk. "Are you new here, sir?" he asked loudly. "Would you like some dessert?"

"Thank you, young man," Veli said, as if he had never seen Jimmie before in his life. "Sit down and talk with me a minute."

Jimmie put his plate on the grass and sat down cross-legged. He looked around as best he could without turning his head. No one seemed to be paying any attention. They ate in silence for a few minutes.

"That's your granddaughter in the green dress, with Cora and Laszlo's sister, Margit," Jimmie said.

"I thought it must be one of those older girls."
Veli nodded and smiled.

"Hey, don't stare at them," Jimmie said in
alarm.

"Sorry." Veli dropped his eyes.

"Cora wants us to show her the locket. I hope
you have it with you. Will you let me borrow it?
But don't be obvious that you're giving me
something."

Veli put his hand in a back pocket and pulled
out a handkerchief. He blew his nose. After he
returned the cloth, he reached into his front
pocket, pulled out the small red box, and let it
slip to the grass beside his leg.

Jimmie picked up their empty plates, and
managed to tuck the box into his own pocket.

"We'll let you know what she says," he said.
Then he walked away.

He threw away the paper plates and put the
dirty silverware in the dishpan where it was
supposed to go. Games were starting to be
organized, and he grabbed Laszlo and ducked
behind a group of adults so they wouldn't be

directed to line up for a relay race. He headed for the parking lot.

Cora was already there with Beth. She looked impatient.

"Have you got it?"

Jimmie nodded.

"What's going on?" Beth asked. "What kind of game are you playing? Was the invitation to come to this picnic just some kind of trick?" She got red in the face, and looked like she might cry.

"Don't be angry, please," Cora said. "We did get Margit to invite you, but she doesn't know why."

"I guess if we tricked anyone, it was Margit," Laszlo said.

"We really do have something to show you," Jimmie added.

"Well, what?" Beth said, at the same time as Jimmie produced the red velvet box.

Cora took it from his hand and opened the lid. Then she snapped open the golden oval case and held the locket out toward Beth.

"Do you know any of these people?" She asked.

Beth touched the smooth gold and ran her finger around the curved edge. She leaned forward to study the small pictures. Then she gasped. "I don't know this couple, but the child on the other side... I've seen that picture. I... I think it's my mother."

18. VELI IS RECOGNIZED

Just then, sounds of cheering reached their ears. The first race must have finished.

Cora's mother appeared around the end of the row of cars. She was looking for them! Cora quickly closed the locket and the case, and handed them to Beth. "It's yours. I'll have to explain later."

Reeta Dubois grabbed Cora's arm. She was annoyed. "There you are. What are you children doing? The games have already started. Hurry up or you'll miss out."

"Oh, Mom. You know I hate racing in a dress," Cora said.

"Nevertheless, we're guests and you'll come join the others." She gave Jimmie and Laszlo each a little push to direct them toward the games area. "Now," she added.

Beth stayed very close to Cora.

Laszlo whispered to Jimmie, "She wants to hear the story about the locket."

"Let's hope we get a chance to tell her," he replied.

They arrived back at the lawn in time for the wheelbarrow race. Since the girls were still in their church dresses, they were the drivers, and the boys had to be the wheelbarrows. They walked on their hands while the girls held their legs and directed them. Cora and Jimmie were a team, and Beth asked Laszlo if he'd be her wheelbarrow. Beth was older than most of the kids in the races, but she seemed to be enjoying herself. They actually won! Laszlo was a very strong boy for his size.

The adults were just getting things organized for the three-legged race, when Jimmie heard a booming male voice say, "Veli Sepannen! You old rascal. I haven't seen you for twenty years."

"Uh oh," Laszlo said.

Beth turned around and stared. "Sepannen? That was my mother's name before she was married."

Cora reached out and took her new friend's hand. "You weren't supposed to find out like this. He wanted to meet you in private, but that man, Veli Sepannen, is your grandfather."

"In private?" Beth asked, her eyes filling with tears. "Is he ashamed of me? Why hasn't he ever visited me before now?"

Jimmie stepped in and patted the girl on the back. He was definitely not used to crying girls, but he thought he had to say something. "He and your mother had a big fight a long time ago. He's afraid she still won't want to see him, but he hitchhiked a long way to get to know you and give you the locket. The people in the picture on the other side are your grandmother and Veli."

"He asked us to help find you because he didn't even know your name," Cora added.

Laszlo said, "He was sick and we helped him get well. Then we figured out who you were as fast as we could."

On the other side of the lawn, a heavy white-haired man Jimmie only knew as Mr. Douglas was pumping Veli's right hand, while holding his shoulder with the other. He was smiling and nodding. Veli, however, looked worried and distracted. A few other adults stood and were walking toward them.

Jimmie took this in at the same time as he was trying to focus on Beth and Cora.

Veli's eyes locked with Jimmie's. Suddenly, Veli dropped Mr. Douglas' hand and pushed his way through the small crowd of people who were gathering around him. He came toward the children.

"Beth?" he said in a quiet voice. "Can you forgive an old grandfather who waited too long to try to find you?"

Beth hesitated only a second. She ran toward Veli and threw her arms around him. "You're really my grandfather?" she asked.

"I really am," he said. "Do you have the locket?"

The girl released Veli and removed the box from a pocket in her dress. She handed it to the man.

"Oh, it's yours to keep," he said. "But open it and look at the pictures."

"I saw the one of my mother. I know that one."

"Good, child. But look at the other one."

Beth opened the locket and studied the other picture. "I think this is you as a younger man," she said.

"It is. And this woman is, was, your grandmother Sonja. She died..."

"Oh, no, I'll never meet my grandma?" Beth said sadly.

"It's true," Veli said, "and I'm sorry. But she made me promise to search for you and try to make amends with your mother. So it's because of her that I have found you."

"You didn't want to find me for yourself?" Beth asked.

"I have always longed to know you, but I was foolish and proud," Veli said.

"What does being proud have to do with anything?"

"I didn't want to admit that your mother, my daughter, might have had a right to be angry with me."

Beth was crying again, "But what did you fight about? It can't have been that important."

Veli shook his head and pulled Beth close to him. He said sadly, "I can't even remember any more."

19. VELI AND OONA

Small towns are known for being places where news travels fast, but this news was passed on at the speed of the lightning in the big storm. The Ramsey house was only a few blocks from the church, and apparently someone who had known Oona Ramsey's maiden name had gone to find her as soon as Mr. Douglas had yelled, "Veli Seppanen."

Jimmie could only assume this was what had happened, because while Beth and Veli were still hugging, a black car sped to the curb and braked quickly, making the car rock on its springs. The doors opened and a man and woman hurried out and ran across the lawn.

The woman grabbed Beth and pulled her away from Veli. "What are you doing?" she demanded.

Beth thought her mother was talking to her and began, "This is grandpa..."

But Oona was looking at Veli with an angry face. "You have no right to come here and talk to my daughter without asking my permission," she accused.

"Oona," Veli said, "Please let me explain. Your mother has died. I would like to forget the past and be a family once again. It's what she wanted most."

Oona took a step backwards. "Mami is dead?"

Veli hung his head. "It was her heart. She didn't suffer. But her death made me realize how foolish I've been to never try to find you. Time is really all we have to share."

"You said Ralph was a bad boy, and that you couldn't let me marry him." Oona stubbornly continued in her anger.

Beth tugged on her mother's arm, "Please, Mom, you're making a scene."

And, indeed, it was a scene. Everyone who was at the picnic had gathered in a circle around Veli, Oona and Beth. Someone must have given Ralph Ramsey a shove, because he took a stumbling step and joined his family in the middle.

"Sir, Mr. Sepannen," Ralph said. "I'd like to apologize to you for a few things."

Oona glared at her husband.

"No, it's all right," he said to her. Then he turned to Veli again.

"I think you knew about some of the wilder things I did when I was a boy. I was a young man headed for trouble. In that you were right."

"Ralph!" Oona exclaimed. "What?"

But Ralph continued talking to Veli. "Your daughter, Oona, is the best thing that ever happened to me. And Beth..." He reached over and pulled the girl close beside him. He seemed unable to continue speaking.

Beth snuggled under her father's arm, but she couldn't take her eyes off her new-found grandfather.

"I grew up in a hurry when I had someone who cared about me. We've lived in Cherry Hill since Beth was born. I have a steady job and a decent house. It's not fancy, but I think I've taken good care of your daughter."

"Yes," Veli said. "I can see you have done that. Thank you."

Veli motioned to Jimmie and his friends, "Come here, children," he said.

Jimmie, Cora, and Laszlo came to Veli's side. Margit held back. She didn't know Veli, and wasn't sure what her brother had to do with it.

Veli then nodded at Reeta and Philippe Dubois. "This all began when some kind people gave me a ride."

Apparently the Dubois' had not recognized Veli without his hat and brown suit. "It's the hitchhiker!" Reeta exclaimed.

He then told everyone the story of how Jimmie had found him in the cabin, and how the three children had nursed him back to health and brought him food. He promised to pay the families back for the supplies the children had taken without permission. He explained how he had then asked them to help him find his granddaughter.

"We're glad to have you back in the neighborhood," Jed Mosher said, stepping forward and shaking Veli's hand. "I remember you from when I was a boy. Consider any food that came from our house a gift."

"Yes, and this one looks just like you," Veli said, gripping Jimmie by the shoulder.

Philippe Dubois agreed that any food taken to a man in need was no problem.

Laszlo did a funny little dance and yelled "Hooray!"

Cora looked up at Veli and pulled on his sleeve. They had a whispered conversation, then Cora motioned for Margit to join them.

Shy Margit shook her head, but Cora went and drew the older girl into the circle.

Cora was not at all bashful, even talking to this large group of adults. "Margit helped too. After my mom told me Oona's last name, then Margit invited Beth to the picnic, so we could talk to her. It took all of us to help Veli meet Beth."

"Welcome back, my old friend," Mr. Douglas said.

This seemed to break the ice and everyone crowded closer, trying to shake Veli's hand and congratulating the children for helping to reunite the Sepannen family.

20. NEW NEIGHBOR

"Why is it called Fishkill Lake?" Jimmie asked Veli. "The fish here aren't dead." The two were standing on the banks of the small body of water behind the cabin, two days after the reunion at the picnic.

"Kill is an old Dutch word for a stream. It's a common name in the East. I'm sure you've heard of the Catskill Mountains in New York. Someone probably moved here from that area. Long before my time."

"So Fishkill Creek got its name first, and then someone found this lake that feeds it," Jimmie said, understanding.

"And the road was built and named last," Veli said, pulling in his line as the bobber disappeared beneath the surface. "Shucks, that one got away."

"You'll get the next one," Jimmie said.

"Might have to rename that road," Veli suggested.

"What? Why?"

"I went to the courthouse yesterday. Thought I'd try to find out who owns this cabin now," Veli said.

"My dad says it's not part of our property."

"Turns out, it's still mine. My Sonja did the household accounts, and she paid the taxes on it all those years. I never knew. Maybe they'll change it to Sepannen Road."

"Yippie!" Jimmie yelled. "Will you stay? Will you be our new neighbor?"

"I will," Veli said. "And I think we'll start being neighbors with a party."

"Are you serious? Here? Can we invite everyone?"

"I already have," Veli said. "Wonder what time it is? I don't have a watch."

Jimmie looked up at the sun. He held his hand out at arm's length and squinted. "About five, I think."

"Good," Veli said. "Also, do you know what day it is?"

"It's Tuesday. Are you getting sick again? You should know it's Tuesday."

"Of course it's Tuesday, but what other day is it?"

"Other day? I don't know," Jimmie said.

"It's your little friend's birthday." Veli winked at Jimmie.

"Cora? Oh, my gosh! Sunday was so exciting that I forgot."

Just then the sound of motors in the woods reached their ears.

"Here come the guests," Veli said.

The Dubois' car, along with the Szep's truck, was pulling into the clearing by the cabin as Veli and Jimmie arrived from the lake. Philippe and Reeta Dubois, with Cora, climbed out of the green Hudson. Jed Mosher jumped from the back of the pickup and Margit handed little sister Eniko down to him. Then she and Laszlo also climbed down. Istvan and Maria Szep, along with Hazel Mosher exited the cab of the old truck. One more car appeared between the trees. It was black.

"It's Beth and her mom and dad," Margit said, and ran to meet her newly-made friend.

Cora waved to Jimmie and called, "I asked Veli if we could have my party here."

"Take some advice, young man," Veli said quietly. "Don't tell her you forgot."

Jimmie grinned up at his friend and new neighbor. Then his face fell. "But I don't have a gift for her."

"Yes, you do. It's all wrapped up on the table inside."

"But, how?"

"Oh, she asked me on Sunday if we could have the party here, and just casually mentioned that she hoped she got some colored pencils. That's from you. I got her some of those new-fangled Magic Markers and a pad of paper."

"I'll pay you back when I get enough allowance money," Jimmie promised.

"Oh, maybe," Veli said. "You kids saved my life, you know. I'm not dirt poor anyway, and

Cora's father offered me a job at the canning factory. I'll need an income to repair this place. Sold my other house; couldn't bear to be there without Sonja."

Dishes loaded with fried chicken were brought from the back seat of the Hudson, along with a huge bowl of potato salad. Philippe and Istvan had already carried the table outside. A picnic jug of Koolaid was unloaded from the back of the truck, along with a grocery sack full of paper plates, cups, and silverware.

Finally, Cora's mother carried a large new Tupperware container from the car and placed it in the middle of the table. She removed the lid and revealed a chocolate cake dotted with confetti sprinkles. Cora's father was right behind her with the Tupperware pitcher Cora had "borrowed," filled with ice tea.

Blankets were spread to cover the edge of the porch, so people could sit without getting splinters.

After everyone was full of good food, and the story of Veli's journey to find Beth had been retold several times, with much laughter and many details added, Veli made a little speech.

"I have come back to the first home I had as an adult. I built this cabin with my own hands, and I intend to repair it with these same hands, although they are old hands now. Sadly, Sonja cannot be with us to see her favorite daughter Oona and the lovely Beth."

Oona wiped a tear from the corner of her eye.

"However, I will do everything in my power to be a good grandfather. And I hope you all will allow me to be an extra grandfather to these resourceful children."

Eniko had been sitting with Margit. Now she went to Veli, reached up and touched his cheek "Grandpa?"

Istvan nodded at Veli and said, "Our parents are all gone. You will be a wonderful grandfather."

Veli lifted Eniko to his knee. Beth came and snuggled into his side. "I hope you will all come visit me often even now that I am well.

"This is the best birthday ever," Cora said. And she hadn't even opened her presents yet.

TELL TIME WITH THE SUN AND YOUR HAND

STAND FACING THE SUN AND EXTEND YOUR ARM
FULLY WITH YOUR HAND TURNED TO PARALLEL
THE HORIZON. SPREAD YOUR FINGERS A TINY BIT.
EACH HANDWIDTH BETWEEN THE SUN AND THE
HORIZON IS ABOUT AN HOUR OF TIME.

TO TELL THE APPROXIMATE CLOCK TIME, YOU
HAVE TO BE AWARE OF SUNRISE OR SUNSET TIMES.
IN THIS STORY, IN FOREST COUNTY IN JULY,
SUNSET WAS AT ABOUT
9:30 PM. SO WHEN THE
SUN WAS 3 HANDWIDTHS
ABOVE THE HORIZON, IT
WAS 3 HOURS EARLIER,
OR ABOUT 6:30 PM, THE
TIME JIMMIE WAS TO
BE HOME.

HORIZON

IN THE MORNING,
IF SUNRISE WAS AT
7:00 AM, AND THE SUN
WAS NOW 2 HANDWIDTHS
ABOVE THE HORIZON,
IT WOULD BE 7+2,
OR 9:00 AM.

THIS WORKS WHETHER
YOU ARE A SMALL CHILD
OR AN ADULT!

WHEN SHADOWS ARE
THE SHORTEST, IT
IS NOON.

Hungarian Cherry Soup

This is a traditional Hungarian recipe for a spicy, cold fruit soup—very refreshing in the summer! You can remove the pits, or have fun spitting them out. Use any kind of tart cherries.

    1 pound tart cherries
    4-5 tablespoons sugar
    2 whole cinnamon sticks
    6 whole cloves
    a pinch of salt
    1 cup yogurt or sour cream
    1 tablespoon flour

Put the cherries with the sugar in 1 quart of water in a large saucepan. When it boils, add the cinnamon and cloves and simmer 10 minutes.

Put the yogurt (or sour cream), salt and flour in a bowl and mix. Add a cup of the hot cherry liquid to this, a little at a time, and stir till it's smooth. Then put this mixture back into the pan with the cherries, stir, and simmer 5 more minutes.

Pick out the cloves and cinnamon (the cloves will float).

Allow the soup to cool, then chill in the refrigerator and serve cold.

ACKNOWLEDGEMENTS

Determining how a Finn might pronounce English words with an accent turned out to be difficult. Assistance was provided by Joan Newman, of Minnesota, whose DNA is 90% Finnish, although she can't imagine where the other 10% came from.

She says, "Finnish people pronounce the first syllable in a word while Americans pronounce the second syllable. Finns also sound out every vowel, so sauna is pronounced 'sownah', not 'sawna' like most Americans do, which drives most Finns nuts when they hear it pronounced incorrectly."

As always, any final errors are the fault of the author.

Joan H. Young, March 2018

OTHER PUBLISHED WORKS
BY JOAN H. YOUNG

Non-Fiction:

North Country Cache: Adventures on a
National Scenic Trail

Would You Dare?

Devotions for Hikers

Fiction:

Anastasia Raven Mysteries:

News from Dead Mule Swamp

The Hollow Tree at Dead Mule Swamp

Paddy Plays in Dead Mule Swamp

Bury the Hatchet in Dead Mule Swamp

Dead Mule Swamp Druggist

The Dubois Files:

listed at the front of this volume

ABOUT THE AUTHOR

Joan H. Young has enjoyed the out-of-doors her entire life. Highlights of her outdoor adventures include Girl Scouting, which provided yearly training in camp skills, the opportunity to engage in a ten-day canoe trip, and numerous short backpacking excursions. She was selected to attend the 1965 Senior Scout Roundup in Coeur d'Alene, Idaho, an international event to which 10,000 girls were invited. She rode a bicycle from the Pacific to the Atlantic Ocean in 1986, and on August 3, 2010 became the first woman to complete the North Country National Scenic Trail on foot. Her mileage totaled 4395 miles. She often writes and gives media programs about her outdoor experiences.

In 2010 she began writing more fiction, including several award-winning short stories. The Hitchhiker is the second book in the Dubois Files mystery series.

Visit booksleavingfootprints.com for more information.